BY
EVELYN LUNEMANN

ILLUSTRATIONS BY
MAX RANFT

FAIRWAY DANGER

BENEFIC PRESS • WESTCHESTER, ILLINOIS

SPORTS MYSTERY SERIES

TEN FEET TALL

NO TURNING BACK

FAIRWAY DANGER

TIP OFF

Editor, Mary Alice Breslin

Library of Congress
Number 68-54058

Copyright © 1969 by Benefic Press
All Rights Reserved
Printed in the United States of America

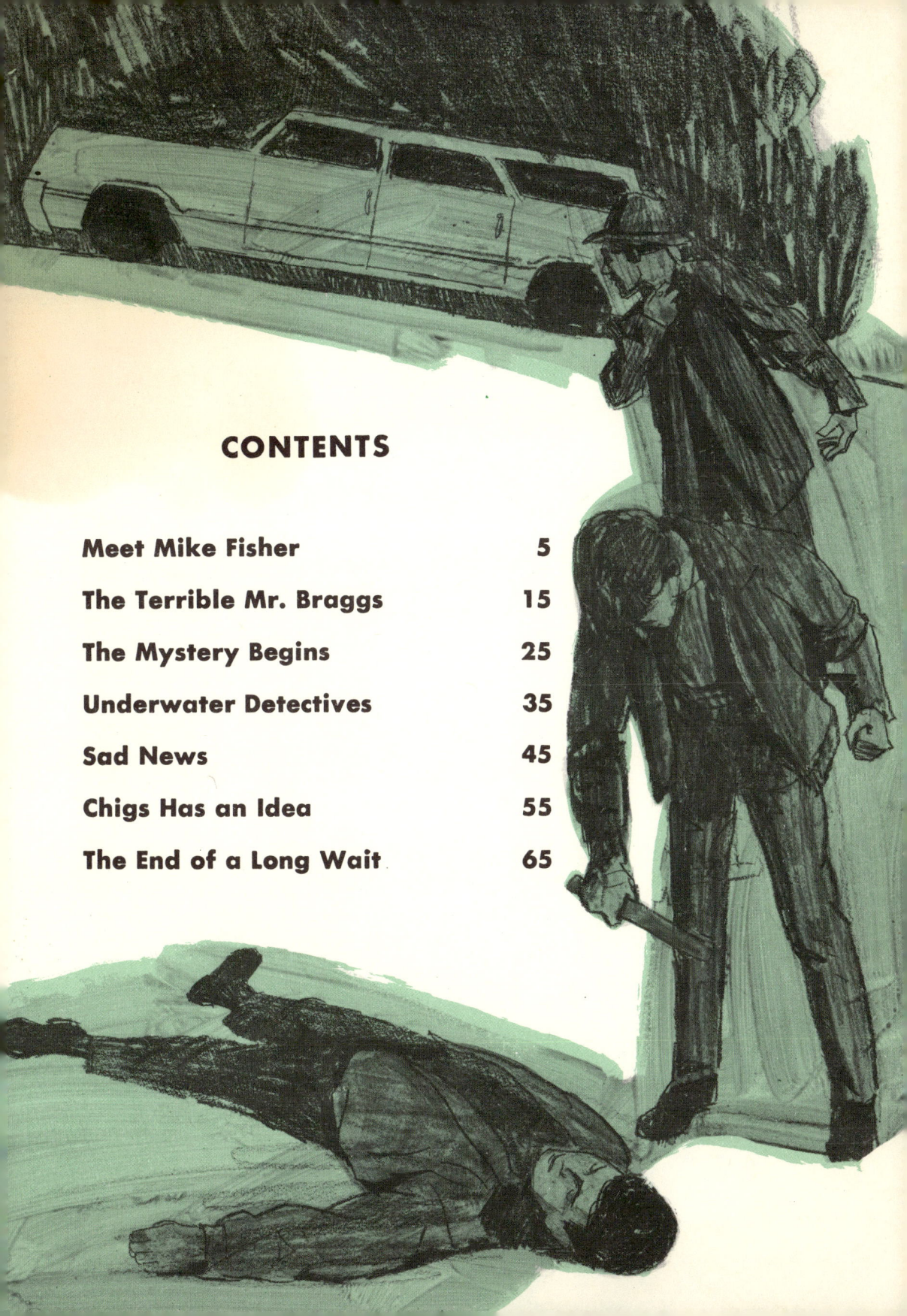

CONTENTS

Meet Mike Fisher	5
The Terrible Mr. Braggs	15
The Mystery Begins	25
Underwater Detectives	35
Sad News	45
Chigs Has an Idea	55
The End of a Long Wait	65

Meet Mike Fisher

Bumps Blake drove his truck up the road that led to the Hickory Hills Golf Course. He looked with pride at the fairways around him. The grass was covered with heavy morning dew. Where the sun slanted through the trees everything was a fresh silvery green. Other places were still in the shade. Such spots were a beautiful dark green.

"It's great to be the 'pro' at such a fine course," Bumps thought to himself. He took a deep breath of the fresh morning air.

As Bumps parked his truck in back of the club house, he looked across the course. Mike should be coming any minute now. He and Mike enjoyed the early morning minutes they spent together. There was little time to talk after the golfers began to come into the club house.

Bumps shaded his eyes as he looked across the course again. Then he smiled. There was Mike running across the fairways. Bumps waved and turned to enter the club house.

Mike Fisher was sixteen years old. He had helped Bumps at the club ever since he was a little fellow. There was a warm friendship between the two. Mike lived with his mother and twin sister. He often did things with Bumps that other boys did with their fathers. Sometimes they hunted or fished. Whenever there was time they played golf together. Some of their best times were when they just talked.

In a few minutes Mike bounded in the front door of the club house. "Hi," he panted. "What a day this is!"

"Good morning," answered Bumps. "It is a beautiful morning. I'd really like to play a round of golf myself on a morning like this."

Mike laughed. "Is there any kind of a day when you wouldn't like to play a round of golf?"

Bumps smiled back at Mike. "No," he agreed, "and I know where I can always find someone who is ready to play with me."

Mike felt happy as he went about his work. He put more score cards on the counter. After that he dusted the shelves. "It's fun to work here," he thought for the hundredth time. He felt lucky to have the job, even though the hours were pretty long.

Mike worked hard and cheerfully for several reasons. Besides the fact that he liked his work and liked Bumps, the money he earned was important to him. Some boys saved for a car or motorcycle. Not Mike. There were two things he wanted more than anything else in the world.

First of all, Mike wanted a set of golf clubs just like the ones Bumps had. There was a set like them for sale at the club house. They hung on the wall where Mike could see them every day. He wanted them so much that he dreamed about them at night.

As he walked past them he stopped and looked up. Carefully he placed his hands as if he were about to swing one of them.

"Why don't you use them?" asked Bumps.

Mike dropped his hands. He felt a little foolish. "No thanks," he said. "I have them about half paid for. I can wait until I have the other half of the money."

"I trust you," said Bumps. "I don't think you'll skip the country if you take them."

"You can't tell about that," Mike said with a smile. "Thanks anyhow. I want to wait until they're mine." He grabbed a broom and started to sweep.

The sun was bright all day. Golfers streamed in and out of the club house. They kept Bumps and Mike busy. It was after dinner before most of the players had gone for the day. Bumps turned to Mike with a sigh.

"Well, Mike, get your sack. Let's go and see how many poor, unhappy golfers there were today."

"The more unhappy players there were, the happier I'll be," answered Mike. "It's just as you say, Bumps. What is good for some people may be bad for others."

"There should be a lot of balls in the river tonight," Mike said as he and Bumps walked across the golf course. "I hope the water has warmed a little bit," Mike continued. He thought again of the diving suit.

Bumps shook his head. He remembered the night before. Mike's friends had stopped at the club house to invite him to a movie. Mike had said, "I'd like to go. If I spend all my money I'll never get my clubs." His friends understood.

One of his friends said, "OK, Mike. I wish I could save my money the way you do."

There was something else that Mike wanted almost as much as he wanted the clubs. He wanted a wet suit for diving. He wanted the suit for fun, and he needed it at the golf course.

The Marshall River flowed through the center of the golf course. It ran between the eighth and ninth holes. Many golfers came into the club at the end of the day and said, "Mike, there's one more down under for you." It was Mike's job to dive for the golf balls at the end of each day. Bumps paid Mike for every ball that he brought up from the river. The river was fed by springs. Even in the summer the water was cold. Many times Mike had said to Bumps, "As soon as I get the clubs paid for, I'm going to start saving for a wet suit. Maybe someday I can even have an air tank and all that goes with it."

Bumps seemed to read his mind. "I think you ought to think of getting one of those new nylon suits. They will last a lot longer than the rubber diving suits. I can get one for you for less money than you would have to pay for it."

"That would really be great," said Mike. "Wouldn't it be fun to dive in the lake up by your cabin? Just think, I could tell you where all the fish were hiding."

"Now you're talking," agreed Bumps.

"I wonder what a person would find in the bottom of a lake like that one," Mike went on. "I'll bet there's all sorts of good things down there." Mike's eyes grew bright as he talked.

"There's one thing you would have to do," said Bumps with a serious look on his face. "Before you go down in that lake, you need to take a course in diving. It doesn't pay to do any diving until you really know how to do it."

"I'm going to take a diving course at the YMCA this fall," said Mike. "You won't have to worry about me, Bumps."

"Good," Bumps answered.

They were nearing the 8th hole when Bumps said with a laugh, "What you need is an overcoat and a pair of mittens tonight. That wind feels chilly."

When they reached the river, Mike threw his sack on the grass. Since he always wore a swim suit under his clothes, he was ready in a minute to dive into the water. Mike was a good swimmer. He wasted no time getting into the water.

"There should be a lot of balls tonight," he said. In a flash he was out of sight. Only some small waves in the water showed where he had been.

It wasn't long until he started throwing the balls out of the water. Sometimes the balls came up one at a time. Sometimes Mike threw up three or four at once.

"This is a good night for you," Bumps called down to Mike. "Looks as though you'll get a lot of them." He helped Mike by putting the balls in the sack.

As Bumps watched, Mike came to the top of the water again. He shook the water from his face and called, "I wish I had that overcoat and mittens you talked about." To himself he said, "What I really wish I had is a diving suit." His teeth were chattering.

"You better come out of the water and warm up," Bumps urged Mike.

They sat on the grass and talked while Mike rubbed his arms and legs. "It's like a different world under the water," Mike told Bumps. "The little fish aren't even afraid of me. Just think what it must be like in a big lake or the ocean. Well," he said as he got up, "here I go, back with the fish."

It wasn't long until Mike called from the top of the water, "I think that's all of them for tonight."

Mike scrambled up the bank. Quickly he slipped back into his clothes. Bumps threw the sack of balls over his shoulder, and the two of them headed for the club house.

It was dusk as Bumps checked the lights and locked the back door of the club house. Mike was washing the last of the mud from the balls. "Look at the good ones we got tonight," he said.

"Let's call it a day," said Bumps.

In a few minutes they left the club house. "See you tomorrow," said Bumps as he locked the door behind them. Mike waved and started across the golf course toward his home.

It took Mike only a little while to cross the golf course and reach his house. "Hi, Mom," he called as he opened the door. There was the smell of fresh baking in the air.

"I'm in the kitchen," called Mike's mother.

As Mike entered the kitchen he stopped in surprise. At the table sat two of his friends. They were busy helping themselves to the cookies Mike's mother had spread on the table.

"I should have known you two would be here if you smelled cookies," laughed Mike.

Howie, the smaller of the two boys said, "We were going to go to the club house and look for you. The only trouble is that they never have fresh cookies there."

The second boy at the table was a huge young man. His name was Chunker. As he reached for a cookie he said, "Would you want us to turn down your mother's cookies?"

"All right, you two," laughed Mike. "What can I eat besides cookies, Mom?"

"I've kept this warm for you," said his mother. "Sit down and eat. You must be starved."

"Thanks, Mom," said Mike as he dug into the food.

"Hurry up," said Howie. "We'll be late for the outdoor show. This is 'buck' night. That's the night for poor guys like us."

A little while later the boys piled into the car.

"I wish it could be summer all year round," said Howie.

"So do I," agreed Chunker, who was driving. "I hope nothing happens to spoil this summer. Remember last summer when I had to hobble around in a cast?"

"Oh, nothing will go wrong this summer," said Mike.

The boys drove off through the summer night.

Mike was to remember his words many times in the weeks that followed.

The Terrible Mr. Braggs

Mike Fisher always spent Thursday afternoons caddying for Mr. Braggs. Mr. Braggs had the biggest house in Center City. He had about the biggest car anyone could buy. He was also one of the "biggest" men who played golf at Hickory Hills.

Mike was the only caddy that Mr. Braggs would have. Whenever he came inside the club house door, even if Mike were in plain sight, he would start to roar, "Mike Fisher! Where is Mike Fisher?"

It was one o'clock when Mr. Braggs came in the club house. "Mike Fisher," he called from the doorway. "Where is Mike Fisher!" Everyone turned to look.

"Here I am, Mr. Braggs," said Mike, who had been standing in plain sight all of the time. "Your clubs are all ready for you."

Mr. Braggs walked over to the golf cart that Mike had pushed out to him. He looked at each club. It was Mike's job to clean the clubs each time Mr. Braggs played with them. Mike really liked to do it because they were such fine clubs.

The clubs must have looked all right to Mr. Braggs. He said, "Well, what are we waiting for? It could start to rain at any time."

Mr. Braggs always thought it was going to rain. He talked about rain even on the brightest days.

Mr. Braggs stamped out to begin his game. Mike waved and smiled at Bumps as he followed behind the big man.

Mike was used to Mr. Braggs. He was used to the way Mr. Braggs always said "Huruumph" every time he hit the ball. That's about all Mr. Braggs ever said.

Par for hole number one was five. Mr. Braggs made it in four strokes. "Huurummph! Birdie! Hurummph!" he said.

On the next two holes Mr. Braggs made one over par. "Hurumph!" he said each time, and almost ran down the fairways.

"How can such a big man go so fast," Mike wondered.

Mr. Braggs was almost smiling by the time he reached the seventh hole. He looked carefully at the sky and then hurried on to tee off for number eight.

"He didn't even say it was going to rain," Mike said to himself. He would like to have told Mr. Braggs that he was playing good golf today. But Mike kept his thoughts to himself. He had learned a long time ago that Mr. Braggs wanted him to say nothing at all.

Mike could not help but smile on the eighth green. Mr. Braggs went down on his knees to line up the ball with the hole. The sight of fat Mr. Braggs with his head down near the ground was almost too much for Mike. Two very good putts on the eighth green brought out a loud "Hurrumph" from Mr. Braggs.

"He really is a good player for a man of his size," Mike thought to himself.

Then to Mike's great surprise, Mr. Braggs started to talk. "This is my day," he said. "Yes, sir. My day. I may make the best score of my life. It all goes to show, my boy. It pays to practice."

Mr. Braggs looked at the river that ran between him and hole nine. He almost smiled.

Carefully Mr. Braggs teed up. After a moment of getting ready, he waggled his club and then swung. Whiff! The club cut through the air. Mr. Braggs looked as if he couldn't believe that his ball was still at his feet.

A sound like an angry growl came from his mouth. Carefully he got himself set for another swing. There was a soft "crack" as the club hit the ball. Up, up went the ball, and then it hooked off to the left. Down it came with a plop into the water.

Mr. Braggs' face was beginning to get red. "Hurrumph!" he grunted. "Ball! Give me another ball." He was almost shouting now. Mike had the ball out and was nearly over to Mr. Braggs when the angry man shouted, "I don't have all day. It could rain at any minute. Hurry up, boy!"

Mike said nothing as he handed another ball to Mr. Braggs. Three times Mr. Braggs leaned down to tee up the ball before it was right. Then he made ready to swing. Two times he changed his stand. Finally he was all set.

Mike held his breath as Mr. Braggs swung. He wanted to close his eyes but knew that he had better watch the ball. "He'll never hit it across when he's like this," thought Mike. Now the ball was in the air. This time it was staying close to the ground. Too close. The other side of the river bank was higher. It would never go over.

Mike held his breath. "It's too low," he groaned.

The ball sailed across the river and hit the opposite bank. It seemed to jump back before it dropped into the water with a loud 'plop'.

"That does it!" yelled Mr. Braggs. "I'm going to fill that river with dirt. Then I'm going to stop playing this fool game."

He ran to the bank. Mike ran after him. Mr. Braggs raised his arms above his head and threw the club in the water. He threw it hard. "You take my balls, so you can take my clubs, too!" he yelled at the river. Before Mike could say a word, he turned around and grabbed the golf cart. He lifted the cart, the bag, and the rest of the balls and threw them into the water.

"Stay there," he shouted. "Stay there forever."

Without even looking back he almost ran along the river to the foot bridge. He headed for the parking lot.

Mike stood with his mouth open. Then he ran after Mr. Braggs. "Mr. Braggs," he called. "Mr. Braggs, let me get your clubs. Please, Mr. Braggs."

"Forget it," Mr. Braggs called to him without turning around. "Leave them for the fish."

Mike ran towards the club house. "I must tell someone about this," he thought. "There should be someone that could talk to him. Those clubs can't stay in the river."

Mike hurried to the club house. Before he opened the door, he could see Mr. Braggs getting into his car.

"Bumps!" Mike called. Then he lowered his voice. It would be best not to tell all the people what had happened.

Bumps was talking to a man about golf lessons. He took one look at Mike and knew that something was wrong.

"It's Mr. Braggs," said Mike in a low voice. "He just threw his clubs and bag and cart in the river."

"In the river?" asked Bumps. "Where is he?"

"He's gone to his car," answered Mike. "What should I do? Should I take them out before he tells me to? He'd really be mad then. We can't leave them there."

Bumps started for the door. "If Mr. Braggs was angry enough to do that, I'm more worried about him than I am about the clubs. He could have a heart attack."

Suddenly the club house door flew open.

"Mike Fisher! Mike Fisher, where are you?" yelled Mr. Braggs. Mike and Bumps turned to see a redfaced Mr. Braggs. He was standing in the doorway. His feet were wide apart. No one in the room said a word. Mr. Braggs looked as if he would go up in smoke at any time.

"My keys," he yelled. "My car keys. Get my keys. They are in that golf bag. They're out there in the water. Don't just stand there. Do you want me to walk home? Maybe you think I can push my car home."

"Yes, sir, Mr. Braggs. Right away," said Mike.

Only Mike and Bumps knew what it was all about. Everyone turned to stare at Mr. Braggs. Mike knew what he had to do. He ran to the door and started for the river. Mr. Braggs puffed along behind him. The golfers and caddies in the club house followed them to the door.

By the time Mr. Braggs reached the river, Mike had his slacks off and was climbing down the bank into the water. It was lucky that Mike always had his swim trunks under his slacks. He swam to the place where he remembered the clubs had gone down.

"It's all right, Mr. Braggs. I found them," Mike called as he came up from his dive. Again and again Mike dived. Each time he brought up a club and handed it to Mr. Braggs.

If Mike had not been so busy he would have seen that Mr. Braggs' face was getting less and less red.

Mike found the golf cart with the golf bag. It was hard to pull them out and up the slippery bank. At last he had them near the top of the bank. Mr. Braggs leaned down to help him. Together they pulled and pushed the cart and golf bag up to the top of the bank.

Mr. Braggs reached into the pocket on the side of the golf bag. "Yep, the keys are here," he said. "You did a good job, Mike."

Mr. Braggs reached for his wallet. "You're a good boy, Mike Fisher. I hope that you learned something today. If I have to tell you what it was, you didn't learn it."

He pulled out two bills and handed them to Mike.

Mike's eyes opened very wide as he looked at the bills. Mr. Braggs was offering him ten dollars.

"Here, boy," he said. "Clean the clubs. And we'd better hurry back before it starts to rain."

"Oh, thanks, Mr. Braggs," said Mike as he looked at the bills in his hand. "Thanks very much."

"Huummph," said Mr. Braggs as he started to walk to his car. "I'll see you in a day or so."

When Mike returned to the club house, he showed everyone the ten dollars and told his story about Mr. Braggs. Some people smiled and some laughed until they cried.

Everyone in the club house was sure of one thing. Mike had earned his ten dollars.

Mike was smiling. "I guess you're right again, Bumps," he said. "A thing may be bad for one person and good for someone else. Earning ten dollars is good for me."

Mike set about cleaning Mr. Braggs' clubs. He was no singer, but today Mike sang to himself. He didn't even care if anyone heard him.

The Mystery Begins

There were only a few golfers left as the sun sank away.

Bumps Blake smiled as he noticed Mike still working on Mr. Braggs' bag and clubs. "Shall we go after golf balls or are you only diving for golf clubs these days?" he asked.

Mike laughed. "No, I think I'll keep diving for balls. I liked the money Mr. Braggs gave me, but I hate to see anyone throw fine clubs like these in the water," he said.

Mike grabbed his ball sack and they started for the river.

He slipped off his slacks for the second time that day and started down the bank of the river. It wasn't long before he had found all the balls. He called to Bumps, "That seems to be all for today. If you have time, I'd like to swim under the bridge."

"OK, Mike," Bumps answered. "Be careful. The water under the bridge is deep."

Bumps picked up the balls that were left on the ground. He walked with the wet sack full of balls over to the bridge to wait for Mike.

Bumps stood alone, enjoying the sunset and the dusk slowly coming over the golf course. Suddenly he thought, "Mike has been under the water for a long time." He went around the end of the bridge to get nearer to the water. He thought he would call to Mike. Then he remembered, "Mike can't hear me when he's under the water." He waited.

Finally Bumps started to take off his shoes. "I'm not much of a swimmer, but I could do something," he said out loud. Just then Mike's head came above the water. He looked as if he had barely made it to the top. He shook the water from his face and swam for the bank.

"What kept you so long?" Bumps called.

Mike took the few strokes that brought him to the bank. He didn't answer until he had climbed out of the water. "Have to rest," he panted.

Bumps waited.

"There are lots of things down there in the deep places," Mike said. "They must have come down after that last high water we had. I wish I had a wet suit. That water is cold. I'd really like to look around. There must be a lot of good things down there."

"Not tonight," Bumps said. "You had me scared. Besides, it's getting dark. Kindly remember that I'm not as good at swimming as you are. When your friend Chigs comes out to the club house, you and he can go down and have another look."

"By the way," he asked, "did any balls drift down that way?"

"Oh, I forgot to look. I really don't know if there were any or not," Mike said.

They both laughed and started for the club house.

"I'm so hungry I could eat eight hamburgers," said Mike as he finished cleaning the club house floor.

"Well, even you should be able to get full of hamburgers for ten dollars," Bumps said.

"Oh, no," laughed Mike. "That ten dollars goes with the money for my golf clubs." He handed the two bills to Bumps. "Here, put them with the rest of the money. I'm going over to Big Burger and get some hamburgers and a milk shake. I'm not going to spend that ten dollars."

"OK," Bumps said as he locked the door. "I'll see you tomorrow, Mike."

"Good night, Bumps."

Mike started across the golf course to the hamburger stand. The shortest way was through the woods beside the golf course. When he crossed the bridge he stopped for a minute to look down at the water.

Mike had three hamburgers and a milk shake. He could have eaten more, but that was all the money he wanted to spend. As he walked back through the woods, he felt happy. The night was warm and the slight breeze felt good. He wanted to do something to show how happy he felt.

All at once he stopped. He heard someone talking. People were not supposed to be on the golf course after closing time. He walked nearer to the river but kept himself hidden in the trees.

"What is going on here?" Mike said to himself. Someone was swimming under the bridge.

Mike dropped down on his knees. He made his way through the grass and small trees. He had to get a closer look.

"There seems to be two of them," thought Mike. "They look more like men than boys. Oh, it looks as if they have wet suits on .... and air tanks. Wow!"

Mike pulled himself nearer the river. There was no sound. "They must be under water," thought Mike. He waited for what seemed to be a long, long time.

"There they are!" Two heads came above the water.

"They do have air tanks on," thought Mike. He could see them wave to each other. "Oh, no!" he said to himself. "They're coming out of the water. They're walking right over here."

They came closer. Mike heard the words, "dead one." "Should I run?" Mike wondered. "No, I'd better stay here and hope that they don't come any closer to me."

When the men were only a little way from Mike they stopped. "Hurry it up," one of them said. "Let's go."

Mike lay very still. He heard them talking to each other in low tones. The words "heavy" and "if he does he'll be dead" came to his ears. Mike felt his body stiffen.

"Should I run?" wondered Mike. "No, I'd better stay here and hope they don't see me."

When they were within a few feet of him they stopped. Mike could not see them but he could hear them. They sounded as if they were almost on top of him.

"Hey," one of them said. "Let's get out of here."

Mike could hear them pulling off their suits. He could hear their breathing as they pulled on their clothes. His own breathing sounded loud to him. He tried to hold his breath.

"Hurry it up," one of the men whispered.

"I'm ready," answered the other one. "The car is over this way. Come on."

"Maybe I should talk to them," Mike thought. "No, Bumps always says there's no use looking for trouble. I'll just be very still."

The men started to walk across the golf course to a car that was parked on the street. They did not say another word. Mike looked hard, but it was too dark to see the car very well. He could not tell what kind it was.

Mike did not move for a little while.

Soon he heard the car start and drive away. "Whew," he said as he got up and began to run through the woods. He panted up to his house.

"What should I do?" he asked himself. "Should I call the police? No, what could they do now. The men are gone. The police may wonder why I didn't run and tell them as soon as I saw the men. It could have been some men that wanted to try out their new wet suits or tanks. But why were they diving at night? Why did they use the golf course? What did they mean when they talked about a 'dead one'?"

"Mom," called Mike as he ran into his house. There was no answer. Then he remembered that his mother and sister were out for the evening.

He sat down to think. There was a funny feeling in his knees and he felt a little ashamed. "Whew!" he said to himself again. "It doesn't take much to scare me." Everything seemed a lot better now that he was here in the lighted living room. "There's nothing the police could do now," he said to himself. "They'll think I was pretty dumb for not running out to check the license number of the car."

Mike tried to get interested in a TV show. His mind kept going back to the men in the diving suits. "Why were they so quiet?" he asked himself. "That's not strange," he answered himself. "No one is supposed to be on the golf course after closing time. Chunker and I were quiet, too, the night we went into the football field when we weren't supposed to be there."

Suddenly he felt hungry. After he had fixed himself a sandwich he felt better. He watched the rest of the show and tried not to think about the men. "I'll tell Bumps about it in the morning," he told himself.

It has been a long day. Mike went to bed. That night he dreamed about swimming in a big lake and diving into a ship that was on the bottom. The whole ship was full of golf balls. What a dream!

Underwater Detectives

In the morning everything seemed better. "I guess that's the way it is," thought Mike. "Things seem more scary at night."

"What do you think about it?" he asked Bumps after he had told the story of the night divers.

"It could have been some kids having fun," Bumps said. "We'll have to tell the police if it happens again. We can't have people on the golf course after closing time."

Late in the afternoon, Mike was still thinking about the divers when something happened to take his mind away from them.

"Hi, everybody!" someone said. They turned around to see Chigs come in the door.

Chigs Moreland was Mike's good friend. Though he was a year older than Mike, Chigs shared Mike's interest in golf. They did lots of other things together in the summer, too.

"Hi, yourself," answered Mike. "It's about time you're getting out on the golf course."

The summer's just begun!" Chigs said with a laugh.

"Why don't you get started right now?" Bumps urged. "Mike has time to play nine holes before clean up time."

"Great!" said Mike. "Let's go, Chigs."

"This is what I've been waiting for," said Chigs.

35

"Where are your clubs?" Mike asked Chigs as he looked around. "I hope you brought them."

Chigs tried to keep the excitement out of his voice as he answered Mike. "My clubs are in the back of the car."

"Car!" asked Mike as he turned to look at Chigs. "What car? Where?"

Chigs' face broke into a wide grin. "Mine," he said. "Come on. I'll show you."

As they went out the club house door, Chigs pointed to a red car in the parking lot. "There she is," he said proudly.

Chigs and Mike hurried over to the car. Mike walked around admiring the automobile. "It's really great," he said as he kicked the tire. "I don't believe it. Let's see the motor."

Chigs was only too willing to raise the hood. "Did you clean the motor up like this? Where did you get it?" Mike asked in a voice that showed he still could hardly believe that Chigs had a car.

"I bought it from the fellow who owns the filling station where I work. He gave me a good deal on it. I can work on it when I'm not busy. I'm going to take the dents out and have it looking just like new."

"Wow!" exclaimed Mike. "I really like this. What did your mother say?"

"Oh, she thought it was all right, as long as I paid for it. Besides, we needed something like this in the family. Now I won't have to carry groceries."

"I'll get my clubs," said Chigs as he opened the trunk. "After we play golf and you get off work, we'll go for a ride."

Mike turned their names into the starter. Then the boys sat down on the bench to wait the few minutes before they could begin their game. There was so much to talk over. Neither of the two boys saw Mike's sister as she came up behind them.

"It must be nice to play golf in the middle of the day," she teased.

Chigs and Mike turned to see who it was. When they caught sight of Mary, they jumped to their feet.

"Hi, Mary," Chigs said. "What are you doing here?"

"Oh, I work here in the club kitchen from now until closing time," she said. "Which reminds me, I'm late. See you later," she called, hurrying toward the club house.

Just then the starter waved them on to the first tee.

"Here we go," said Chigs. "Hope I'm not too much out of practice."

Mike and Chigs were so busy talking and playing golf that it wasn't until they came to Hole 8 that Mike thought about the night divers. He told Chigs what had happened.

"This we have to see about," said Chigs. He was always ready for anything. "We will have to check this out. If it's all right with Bumps, I'll help you dive for balls tonight. Then we'll have time to look under the bridge. Maybe we'll find something really good. I don't want to find a dead body, but I'd like to find something. Come on, let's play this last hole. You've got me beat for today."

The idea that Chigs and Mike go after balls together was all right with Bumps. "Most of the players have gone to dinner. You two can dive for balls now," he said.

On the way to the river, the boys talked about the two divers that Mike had seen.

"Oh, I would hate to find a body down there," said Mike.

"Me, too," said Chigs with a shiver. "Aw, things like that only happen in books or on TV. Maybe we will find some good junk down there."

It didn't take the boys long to find all the golf balls.

Chigs shivered as he came up for air. "It really is cold. This river must have a lot of springs in it to keep it this cold. I can see why you want a suit for diving."

"Oh, I want it for going after balls, but I want it for other diving, too," answered Mike.

"Do you still want to dive under the bridge?" asked Chigs.

"Oh, sure," answered Mike. "Let's walk over, though. That way we can get warm on the way."

39

The boys dropped their sacks of golf balls at the side of the bridge. They slid into the water and dived down. The water was deep. By the time they reached the bottom, they had little air left in their lungs.

There were shelf-like places on the sides of the river bottom. Here the river must have worn away some of the layers of limestone and sandstone. Old logs and huge stones lay in a crazy pattern across the bottom. Mike pointed out something that was shiny metal. They were both out of breath and neither could see what it was. They rose to the top, took a few gulps of air, and dived again.

They headed for the shiny metal again. Together they pulled it out from under a log. It was a hub cap. When they had thrown it up on the bank Mike said, "Well, that wasn't much of a find."

"We can get a few cents for it," said Chigs. "Come on. Let's go down again before it gets too dark."

This time the boys saw only old tires, until Mike spotted a fishing reel. At almost the same time Chigs saw an old, battered fishing tackle box. When he tried to lift it he found that it felt heavy, even in the water.

"What do you suppose is in it?" asked Chigs as he helped Mike carry it up the bank. "It's really heavy."

"It must be lead," panted Mike.

"It's not very old," said Chigs as he unsnapped the cover. "Hey, it is lead. Two bars of it. It looks like that stuff they use to make weight belts for skin diving."

"Well, what do you know?" cried Mike. "Maybe we can make some weights out of it. Weight belts are not cheap when you have to buy them." He turned to look at an old tin can on the grass. "Did you bring that up?"

"Yes," said Chigs. "There's something in it, too. Listen to it rattle."

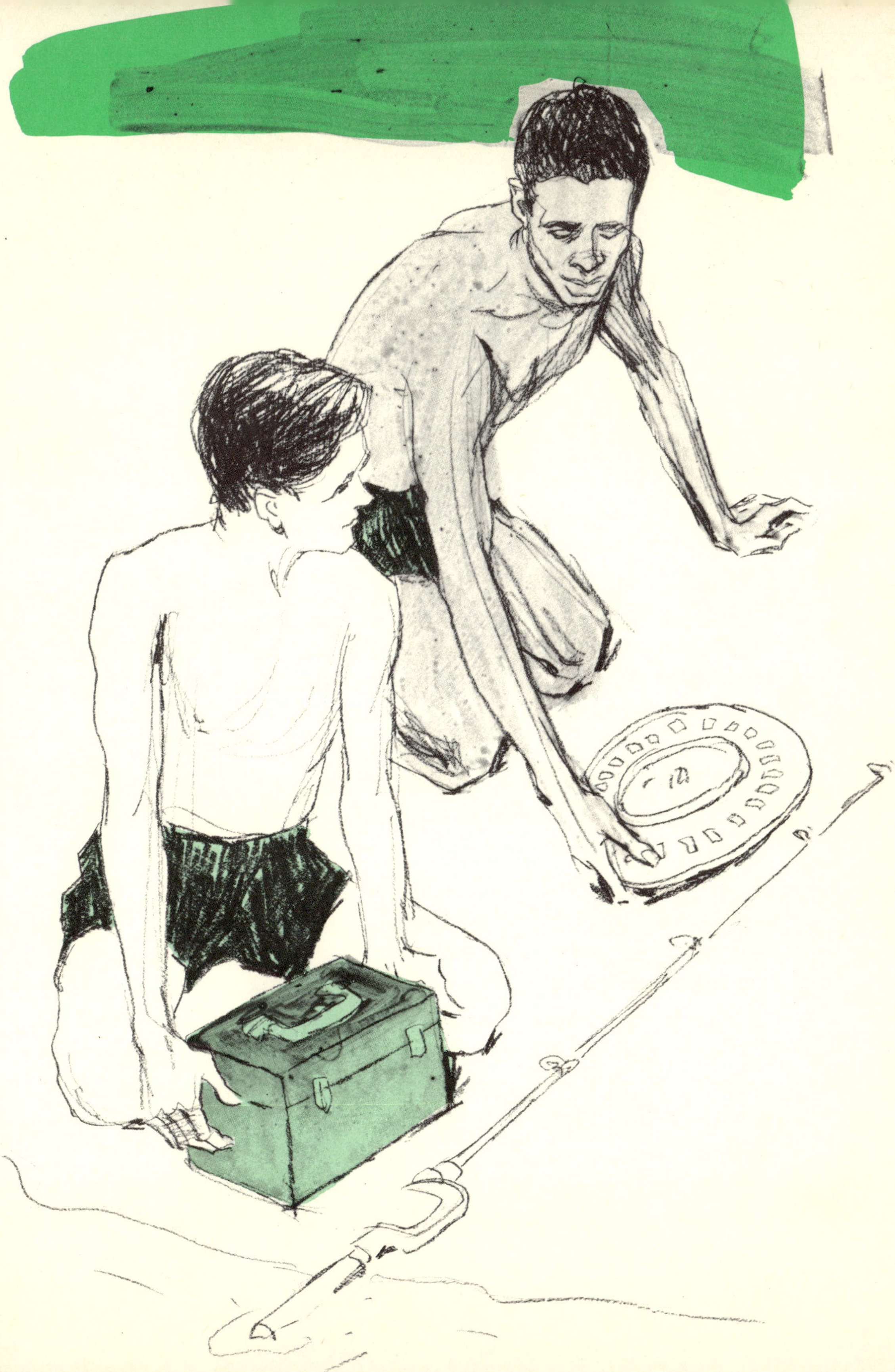

"Open it," said Mike.

"Look," said Chigs as he forced the cover open. "It's lead nickels .... slugs."

The boys laughed. "We haven't found much!" said Mike. "At least we didn't find any dead bodies. That fishing reel isn't too bad."

"Let's quit for tonight," suggested Chigs. "I'm cold. By the time we get back to the club house it will be dark."

Bumps smiled as he saw the two boys dragging in their finds.

"What have you two hunters found?" he asked as the boys came into the club house. "You look as if you had been to a junk yard."

"We didn't find any dead bodies," said Mike.

"I'm glad of that," answered Bumps. "What's in that fishing tackle box? You're carrying it as if it were heavy."

"It is, believe me," said Mike as he set it down. "It's as heavy as lead and that's what it is. Someone must have been going to melt it down into fish line sinkers."

"All that work for this junk," sighed Chigs. "Oh, it was fun anyway. Besides we can sell this hub cap."

42

"I'm glad that you didn't find a dead body, but some money would have been all right," Bumps told them. "You could melt those lead bricks down and make them into lead nickels."

Mike reached into his pocket for the can he had found. "Oh, we already have some of those," he said.

"Why couldn't you have found something that was useful?" Bumps asked them with a smile. "Wait! We can put these lead bricks in the bottom of the golf ball basket. That basket is always tipping over. At last, we can use something that you found."

They were still laughing as they put the lead bricks in the bottom of the tall basket. Later Mike and Chigs poured golf balls over them.

"I hope those divers don't come back," Bumps said. "If they do and you two have to go and check on them, we'll have this place full of junk."

Mike started for the broom.

"Why don't you run along," suggested Bumps. "We can clean up in the morning."

"OK, see you tomorrow, Bumps," called Mike.

"Right," answered his friend.

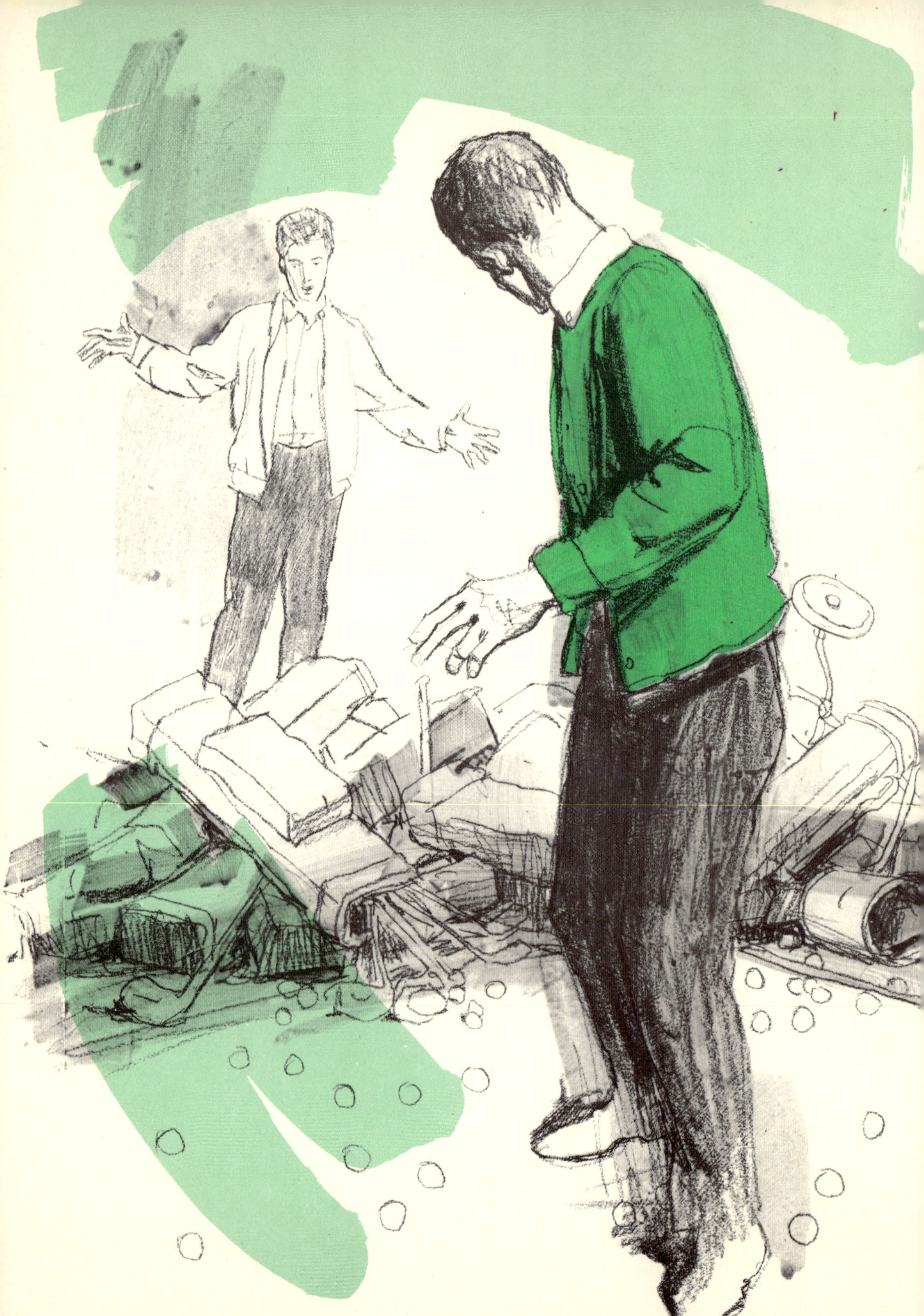

Sad News

The next morning Bumps and Mike walked up to the club house door at the same time. Bumps unlocked the door and started to go inside. He stopped so fast that Mike bumped into him.

"Sorry ..." Mike started to say. Then he looked and stopped in the middle of the word.

The club house was a wreck. Chairs were turned over. Golf bags were dumped everywhere. There were new golf balls and golf tees all over the floor. It looked as if someone had pulled everything out of place.

"Oh, no!" Bumps cried. "Look at this place!"

He reached for the phone and called the police. "This is Bumps Blake over at the Hickory Hills club house. Someone has taken this place apart. They must have been looking for money ... Thanks, I'll be here."

"Don't touch a thing until the police get here," he told Mike after talking to the police. "Look around and see if you can tell what is missing."

It was only a few minutes before the police came.

"Say, this place looks like a wind storm hit it," said Police Officer Crane. "What did they take? Did they get any money?"

"None," Bumps answered. "We never leave any money here overnight. We can't see that anything is missing."

"That's right. Everything seems to be here," Mike added. "But it's such a mess that it's a little hard to be sure. Maybe someone scared them off before they found what they were after."

"How did they get in?" asked one of the other policemen.

"The back door has been opened," Bumps told him. "Whoever it was knew how to open locks, because that door had a good lock on it."

They kept searching all day, but could find nothing missing. It took every spare minute to put everything back in its place. It was dark when they finished.

"Well, that is that," said Mike as he took a look at the clean club house. "This has been a busy day. I'm tired from answering all the questions people asked us. I wish I knew some of the answers."

Officer Crane stopped by just as Bumps and Mike were closing for the day. "It must have been someone that wanted to make life hard for you by making a mess. It could be that they wrecked the place because they were angry over not finding any money. Can you think of anyone who would want to give you trouble?" he asked.

"Mike and I have tried but we can't think of anybody that would want to do anything like this. I hope whoever did it is as tired as we are tonight," Bumps said.

"If you think of anything that would help us, be sure to call," said Officer Crane. "We'll check back with you."

Bumps said "goodnight" to Mike and watched him walk across the golf course toward his home. Then he headed for his truck. As he started the engine he sighed and thought, "I hope this is the end of our trouble."

About 11 o'clock that night, the telephone rang at Bumps' apartment. It was Mike's mother. "Have you seen Mike?"

"No, Mrs. Fisher," he answered. "Mike left the club house an hour ago. Isn't he home yet?"

"No, he isn't home and he hasn't called," she said. "That isn't like Mike."

"Did you try calling Chigs' house?" he asked.

"Yes, I called there before I called you. Chigs went to the late show, but not with Mike," she said.

"I'll call around and see what I can learn," he told Mrs. Fisher. "He may have thought he told you where he was going. I'll call you as soon as I learn anything," he promised.

Bumps didn't know where to look for Mike. He called a few of Mike's friends, but none of them had seen him all evening. He called the Big Burger, but they said Mike had not been there that night.

By 1 o'clock there was still no sign of Mike. Mrs. Fisher and Bumps decided to call the police.

There seemed to be nothing to do but wait. Morning came and they were still waiting. Bumps went to the club house. He didn't know what else to do.

As the golfers began to stream in, many of them asked, "Where's your right hand man, Bumps?" They felt very bad to hear the news.

Bumps sat down at his desk. He started going over everything that Mike had said and done the day before.

"When Mike left last night he had said he was going home," he thought. He traced Mike's route in his mind.

Suddenly he had a thought that made him feel cold all over. "Mike had to cross the river on his way home. Did he slip and fall off the bridge?"

Bumps quickly picked up the phone and called the police. Officer Crane was on duty. He said he would be right over.

As Bumps was hanging up the phone, Chigs appeared at the door of the club house. Chunker and Howie were with him. "Is there any news of Mike?" they asked.

"We haven't heard a word," Bumps told him. "I'm glad that you're here. I'm going to walk across the course the way Mike started to walk home last night. I don't want to think about it, but maybe Mike slipped into the river somehow."

"Mike is too good of a swimmer to have anything happen to him in the river," said Chunker.

"My swim trunks are in the back room," said Chigs. "I'll put them on and then I'll have a look in the water."

They had just reached the bridge when Officer Crane came. As he walked across the course, Chigs slid into the water.

"I can't see how Mike could have fallen into the water," Bumps said. "In the first place, Mike is too smart to be careless. In the second place, he's a fine swimmer. Even if he did fall in, he could take care of himself."

No one said much as they stood waiting.

It seemed like a long time before Chigs came up for air. He shook his head. He took at least a dozen more dives. He looked under the bridge and on each side of it.

At last he came out.

"The water is clear and I can see well under there. It looks the same as when Mike and I were under the other day," panted Chigs.

Bumps felt happier than he could ever tell anyone, but that didn't help find Mike.

"Let's see," Bumps said. "Where would he go after he left the bridge?"

"The shortest way is right through the woods," Chigs said. "We've all gone that way a lot of times. I'll show you."

They had walked into the woods only a short way when Chigs cried out in a voice that didn't sound like his own, "Oh, no-o!"

Officer Crane and Bumps ran ahead of Chigs. There lay Mike -- face down in the grass.

"He's hurt!" Bumps shouted. "He's hurt!"

"It can't be!" said Howie.

There was dry blood on the back of Mike's head. They turned him over carefully. He was so white.

"How could he be alive and be so very white?" Bumps thought. He felt for a heart beat. Yes, it was there. At least he was still alive.

Policeman Crane had already started for his car.

"I'll radio in and get help," he called back as he ran.

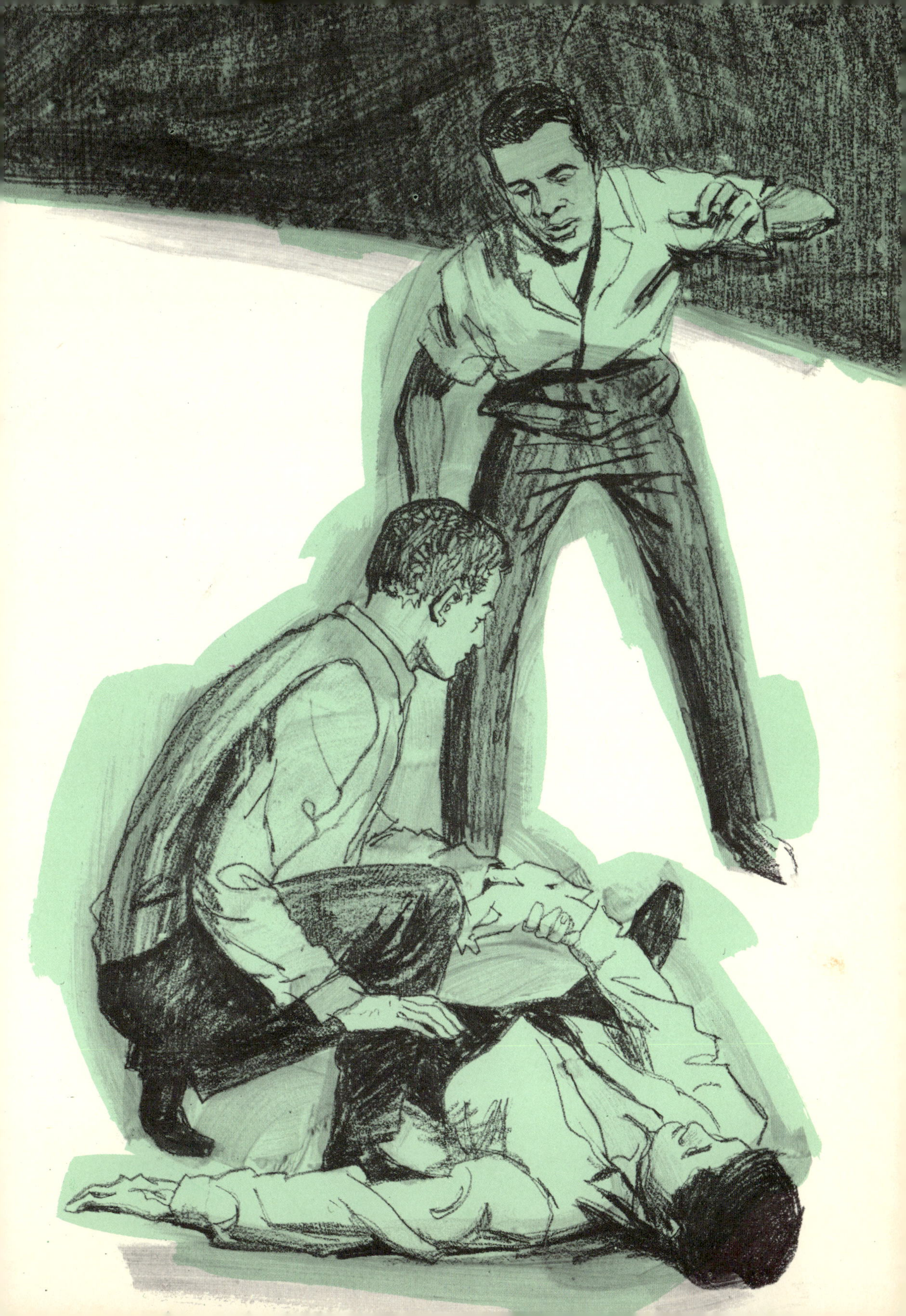

Bumps ran to Mike's side.

"Look at him, Bumps. Look at him. Will he be all right, Bumps?" asked Chigs in a tight voice.

"He just has to be all right, Chigs," Bumps said.

All at once Bumps was angry and scared all at the same time. "Who could have done such a thing to Mike?" he asked himself as he covered Mike with his jacket.

The sound of the sirens came through the woods. Help was coming. In no time white-coated men were running across the golf course.

They lifted Mike carefully on a stretcher and carried him across the course. Bumps and Chigs walked beside them and then rode with them to the hospital.

Officer Crane had stopped to get Mrs. Fisher. They all met at the hospital.

"You'll have to wait outside his room until the doctor has finished his examination," the nurse told them.

After what seemed like a long time, the doctor appeared.

"Mike has not opened his eyes or said a word. He had a very bad bump on his head. There's nothing to do but wait," the doctor said.

Bumps stood up. "I must get back to the golf course." He hated to leave.

"Chigs, can you stay here with Mrs. Fisher?" Bumps asked.

"Sure, Bumps," Chigs said. "I'll call you the minute there is any news. Right now I'll call Howie or Chunker."

Officer Crane had also been waiting. "I'm going, too, Bumps," he said. "We've got to make sense out of this."

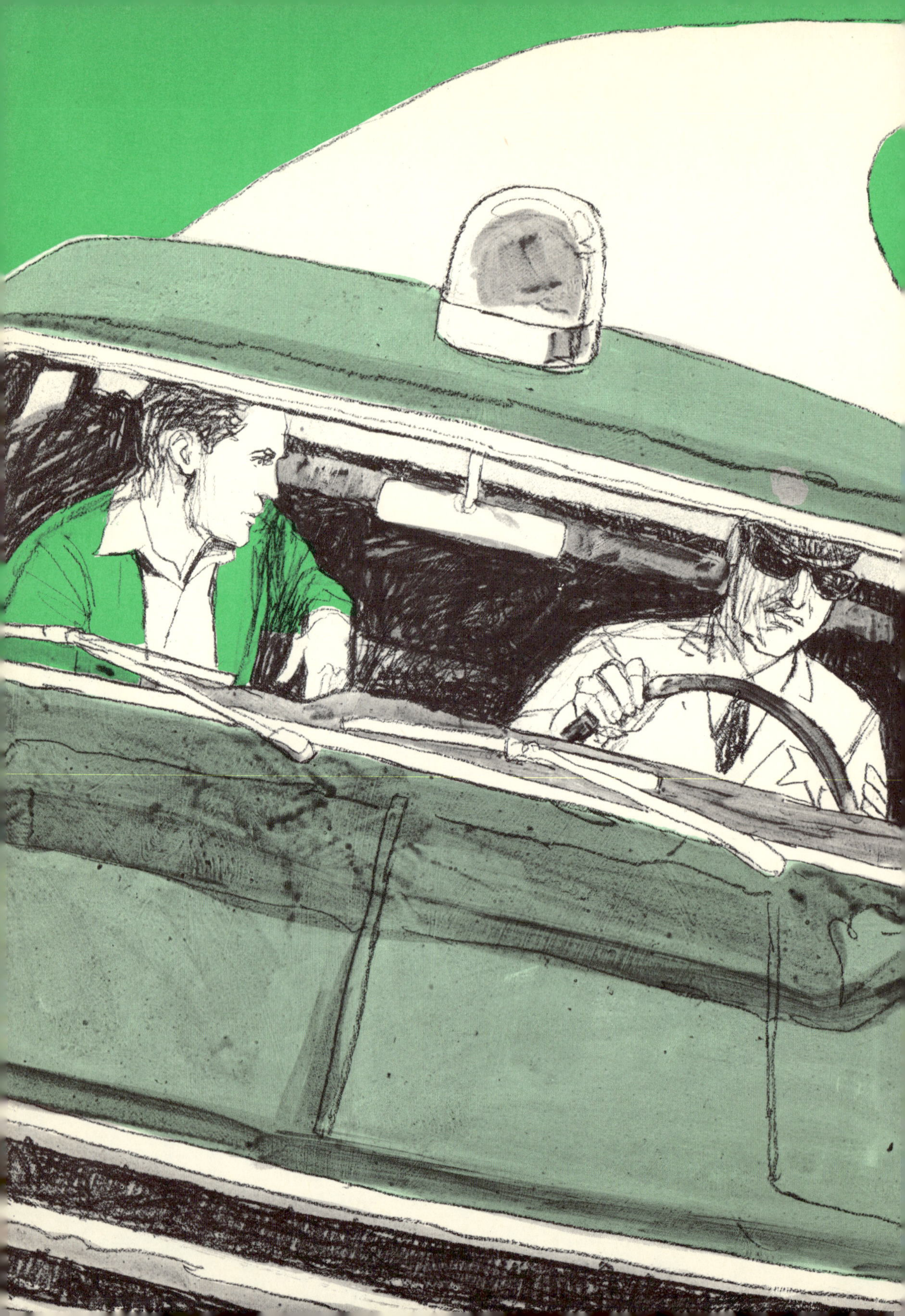

Chigs Has an Idea

As they drove up Slater Street toward the golf course, Officer Crane said to Bumps, "Do you think what happened to Mike has anything to do with what happened at the club house the other night?"

"Why, I never thought about the two things together," Bumps said. "Of course I don't understand either one of them. It doesn't make sense to tear up the club house and it doesn't make sense for someone to hit Mike."

"Are you sure Mike doesn't have any enemies?" asked Crane.

"No, Mike is everyone's friend," Bumps answered.

"Do you think whoever was in the club house that night was looking for money?" asked Officer Crane.

"They must have been," Bumps nodded his head. "When they didn't find anything in the money box, they must have been angry and wanted to do something mean."

"Have you ever seen any strange people around the club house?" asked Officer Crane.

"Sure, there are a lot of strange people around all the time," Bumps said. "There haven't been any strange-acting people around, if that's what you mean."

Bumps tried again to remember anything that would help make sense out of what had happened. He thought until his head seemed to hurt from thinking.

Suddenly Bumps remembered Mike's story about the night divers. "Mike said he saw some men diving under the bridge one night. But I don't see what they could have to do with the club house or with Mike. They didn't see Mike. Chigs and Mike went diving there the next day. They didn't find anything that would interest anyone."

"What do you think the divers were doing in the river?" Officer Crane asked.

"We thought they must have been trying out some new suits or tanks," Bumps said with a shrug of his shoulders.

"This is a strange case, all right. Call me if you get any new ideas that might help us," said Crane.

As the day went on, Bumps listened for the phone to ring. He hoped someone would call to report that Mike was better.

The phone did not ring, but sometime later Chigs arrived at the club house. "They said there wasn't anything I could do at the hospital. Mrs. Fisher thought I should come over here and see if I could help do Mike's work. She will call if there is any change in Mike," said Chigs.

"I'm glad to have you," Bumps said. "I can use some help. While you're working, try to think of anything or anybody strange that you have seen around here. I've thought and thought, but I can't come up with any answers."

"I've been thinking, too," Chigs said. "Do you think that anyone would hit Mike and try to rob him? A lot of people knew that Mike had ten dollars that Mr. Braggs had given to him."

"Oh, how could anyone hit a person for ten dollars?" Bumps asked. "Anyway, Mike had given that money to me. I don't think anyone else knew that, of course. All I hope is that Mike gets well, and then I hope the police find the men who did it."

After they had closed the club house, Chigs and Bumps stopped at the hospital to see if there had been any change in Mike.

"He's just the same," his mother said sadly.

A policeman was waiting with Mrs. Fisher to ask Mike some questions, but Mike had not opened his eyes or made a sound.

"Is there anything we can do?" Chigs asked her.

"Thank you, I can't think of anything that anyone can do. I only wish the police could find the men who did this to Mike, before they hurt someone else."

Chigs and Bumps said goodbye to Mrs. Fisher. There was nothing they could say or do to make her feel better.

Bumps drove Chigs home. They spoke very little along the way. Both were deep in thought.

Later that night Bumps picked up the evening paper. As he started to read, he heard footsteps outside his door. The door opened before he could get to it.

It was Chigs and he had the evening paper in his hand.

"Bumps, don't think I'm crazy but look at this!" He pointed to a story on the inside of the paper.

> Silver Still Missing -- Calgary, Canada
>
> Police have found all but two of the silver bars that were stolen from the silver shipment on April 15.
>
> Police have been unable to find the men believed to have stolen the silver.

"Do you think the bars we found in the river could be silver and not lead?" asked Chigs. "I know it sounds crazy, but that would be a reason for someone tearing the club house apart. They may have seen us when we carried the bars to the club house."

"Chigs, you've been watching too much TV. How would the men who took the silver get it way down here?"

Bumps reached for his coat and put it on as he talked.

58

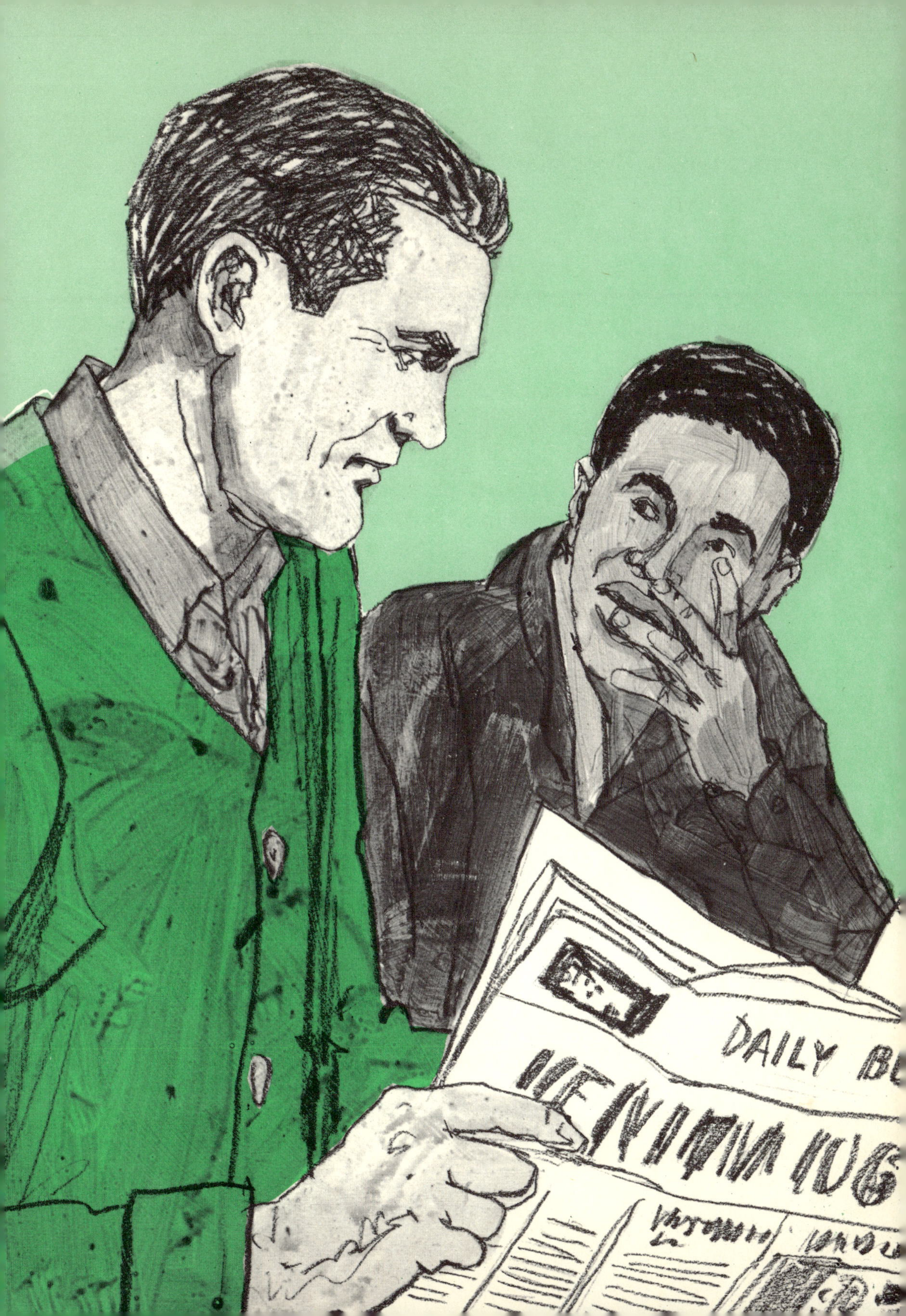
DAILY

"Come on," Bumps said. He was getting excited in spite of himself. "It won't take us long to check on the bars. Then we can have a good laugh at ourselves."

They jumped in the car. As they turned the corner near the club house, they saw lights on in the building. Cars were parked there, too. The door of the club house opened and two policemen came out. They had two men between them.

"What's going on here?" Bumps asked as he hurried to meet them.

"Hello, Bumps. Hi, Chigs," said Officer Crane. "We caught them. We thought they'd be back. Our men have watched this place ever since Mike was hurt. We'll take them downtown and find out what they were looking for. We don't know what it is all about, but we will."

Bumps turned to Chigs. "You'd better tell them why you and I are here," he said.

Chigs walked over to the basket of golf balls. He dumped them over on the floor. The bars were in the bottom.

"What in the world..." shouted Officer Crane as he looked in the basket. "Where did you get these? I'll say these could be what those men were looking for! Why have you been hiding them?"

At that second Officer Crane stepped back. His foot slipped on one of the golf balls and down he went! Bumps stepped over to help him. The next thing he knew, he had slipped, too. There they sat on the floor with golf balls rolling all around them.

"Come on, somebody tell me what's going on around here," said Officer Crane.

Bumps looked at Chigs who was busy trying not to laugh at the two of them on the floor.

"It's like this," Bumps started to explain. "After Mike saw those men diving in the river, he and Chigs went diving, too. They wanted to see what was down there. They thought those men might have left a dead body down there. They didn't find anything except a hub cap, some junk, and these bars. We thought the bars were lead. It was tonight that Chigs read in the newspaper about the silver bars that had been stolen. We were on our way over here to have a look at them."

"Lead bars!" cried Officer Crane. "Do you know how much money you have been using to hold down your golf ball basket?"

"It was a good hiding place, wasn't it?" said Chigs as he began to laugh.

"Now we know what those men were looking for," said Officer Crane. "They must have been watching when the boys went diving. When they didn't find the bars on their first try, they came back to look again."

"Do you think they are the ones who hit Mike?" Bumps asked.

"We'll find out about that when we get them downtown," said Officer Crane. "If they did, let's hope for Mike's sake that they aren't sent up on a charge of robbery and murder."

Officer Crane got to his feet cautiously. "Be careful where you walk, boys," he said. "This is a very unsafe place."

"I'm going to stop over at the hospital again," said Bumps. "Want to come along?" he asked Chigs.

"Yes, I'd like to."

"I'm going to try to get Mrs. Fisher and Mary to go home. They have to get some rest," Bumps said.

"Let's see if they'll let me stay at the hospital," Chigs said.

Chigs and Bumps found Mrs. Fisher and Mary sitting beside Mike's bed. They both looked sad.

"Mrs. Fisher," said Bumps. "You need to get some rest. I've talked to the head nurse. They've agreed to let Chigs stay in the room tonight. Let me take you and Mary home."

"Thank you, Chigs. We'll see you tomorrow," Mrs. Fisher said as she and Mary left the room.

"It feels good to be outside," Mary said. "I guess it's a pretty night...or it would be if Mike were only well."

"He's going to be all right," Bumps said as they got into his truck. "I know he will be. Mike is tough."

They rode in silence for a time.

"Oh, I almost forgot," Bumps said when they were nearly home. "The police may have found out who hit Mike and why." Quickly he told Mrs. Fisher and Mary what had been found at the club house.

They had reached Fishers' house.

"Thanks for taking us home," said Mary.

"And thanks for helping us think that Mike is going to be all right." Mrs. Fisher turned and waved a goodnight to him as she and Mary walked to the door.

Bumps drove slowly home. "He's got to be all right," he kept saying to himself.

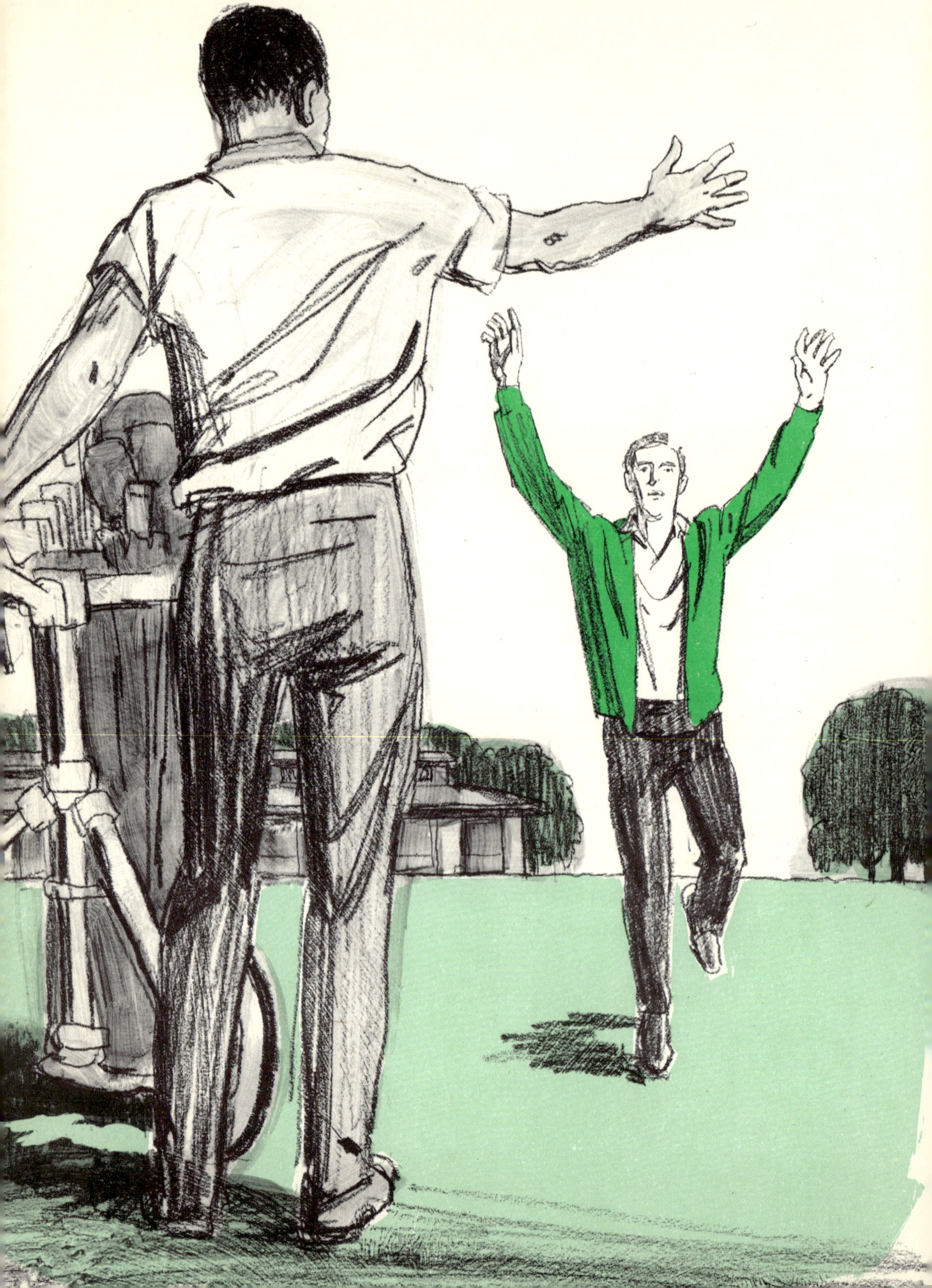

The End of a Long Wait

The next day seemed to pass very slowly for Bumps and Chigs. Mrs. Fisher and Mary had arrived at the hospital early so that Chigs could help Bumps out at the club house.

At about eleven o'clock Mr. Braggs came in. "You, young man," he said as he pointed to Chigs. "You can caddy for me?" It was more like an order than a question.

"Yes, I'll take Mike's place," Chigs answered him.

Mr. Braggs played only four holes and then quit.

Chigs thought it was strange that Mr. Braggs did not ask about Mike. "He must have read the paper," Chigs thought. "Oh, he knows about Mike all right. He didn't yell for him the way he usually does. Of course, Mr. Braggs doesn't worry about anyone except Mr. Braggs."

He pulled Mr. Braggs' cart toward the club house door. He had almost reached it when Bumps came running toward him. One look at Bumps' face told Chigs the story.

"He's better," Chigs heard himself shout. "He is, isn't he? Isn't he?"

"Yes, he sure is," smiled Bumps. He tossed his hat into the air. "Mrs. Fisher said Mike is awake and hungry."

"Whew! That's the best news I've heard," announced Chigs. "When can we go to see him?"

"We can see him for a little while anytime. This day can't go fast enough for me," said Bumps.

65

Chigs cleaned Mr. Braggs' clubs as fast as he could. He even forgot to feel angry at Mr. Braggs. Next he grabbed a broom and swept the club house. Then, just because it was such a wonderful day, he mopped the floor, too.

"That looks fine," laughed Bumps when he saw the wet floor. "Why don't you go over and see Mike. I'll close up here. Tell him I'll be over to see him as soon as I get through. It won't take me long."

"Yes, sir," said Chigs. He raced out the door. When he reached the hospital, he took the steps two at a time. He noticed Mr. Braggs coming down the hospital steps. Chigs was surprised but thought no more about it.

Mrs. Fisher and Mary were just coming out of Mike's room. "He's been asking about you," Mrs. Fisher said. "The doctor is with him. Won't you come with us to the waiting room? A nurse will call us when the doctor has finished. Isn't it wonderful?"

Chigs looked from Mrs. Fisher to Mary. "It's the best news in the world. I'll wait with you until we can go in and see him."

They were still waiting when Bumps came looking for them. "There you are," he said. He shook Mrs. Fisher's hand, "I knew he had to be all right, Mrs. Fisher, but I'd like to hear it from the doctor."

At that minute Officer Crane joined them.

"Have you talked to Mike?" asked Bumps.

"Yes," the officer said. "He was able to tell us some of what happened. Two men grabbed him as he walked across the golf course. They dragged him into the trees and asked the same question over and over. 'Where did you put it?' they kept saying. Mike didn't know what they were talking about. He broke away from them and started to run. That's when one of them hit him."

"I suppose they got scared when they thought they had killed him." Bumps made his hand into a fist. "I'd like to get my hands on them..."

Mike's mother put her hand on Bumps' arm. "It's all over now," she said. "I don't care about anything except that Mike is going to be well again."

The door of Mike's room opened and the doctor came out. He smiled as the small group came toward him. "Your son is doing fine, Mrs. Fisher. His body is in good shape. That helps at a time like this. With lots of rest and quiet he will be as good as new. He shouldn't have too many visitors at one time. Make your visits short."

"Thank you, Doctor Michaels," nodded Mrs. Fisher. She turned to Bumps and Chigs. "I know he'll want to see you. Why don't you two go in."

Bumps and Chigs walked quietly into Mike's room. A dim light was on. Mike lay straight and still under the white sheet. His eyes were closed. When he opened them he smiled slowly. "Don't be so quiet," he said.

Bumps was at his side in one big step. "You're the one that has to be quiet," he said in a loud voice. He caught himself and lowered his voice. "Now don't you say a word. You had us scared to death. Do you know that? Everything is all right now, though. Just you take care of yourself. Chigs is doing such a good job that you can take a long rest."

Mike looked at Chigs and smiled.

"You look fine," said Chigs. To himself he thought, "I don't know what to say. I feel so happy but I don't know what to say."

Bumps started toward the door. "You wait here, Mike...I mean...I know you aren't going anywhere. What I mean is..." He stepped outside the door and returned with a big box.

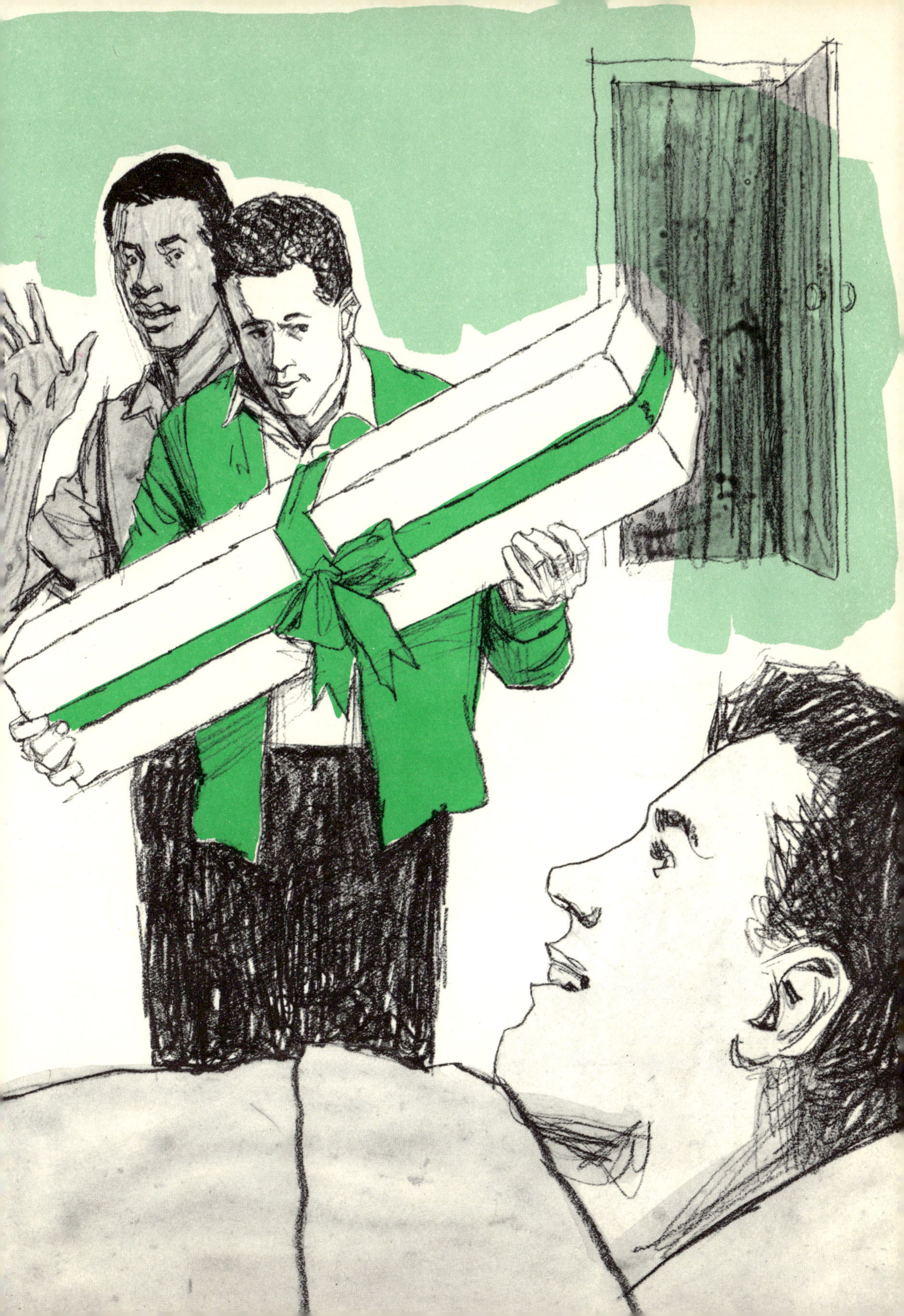

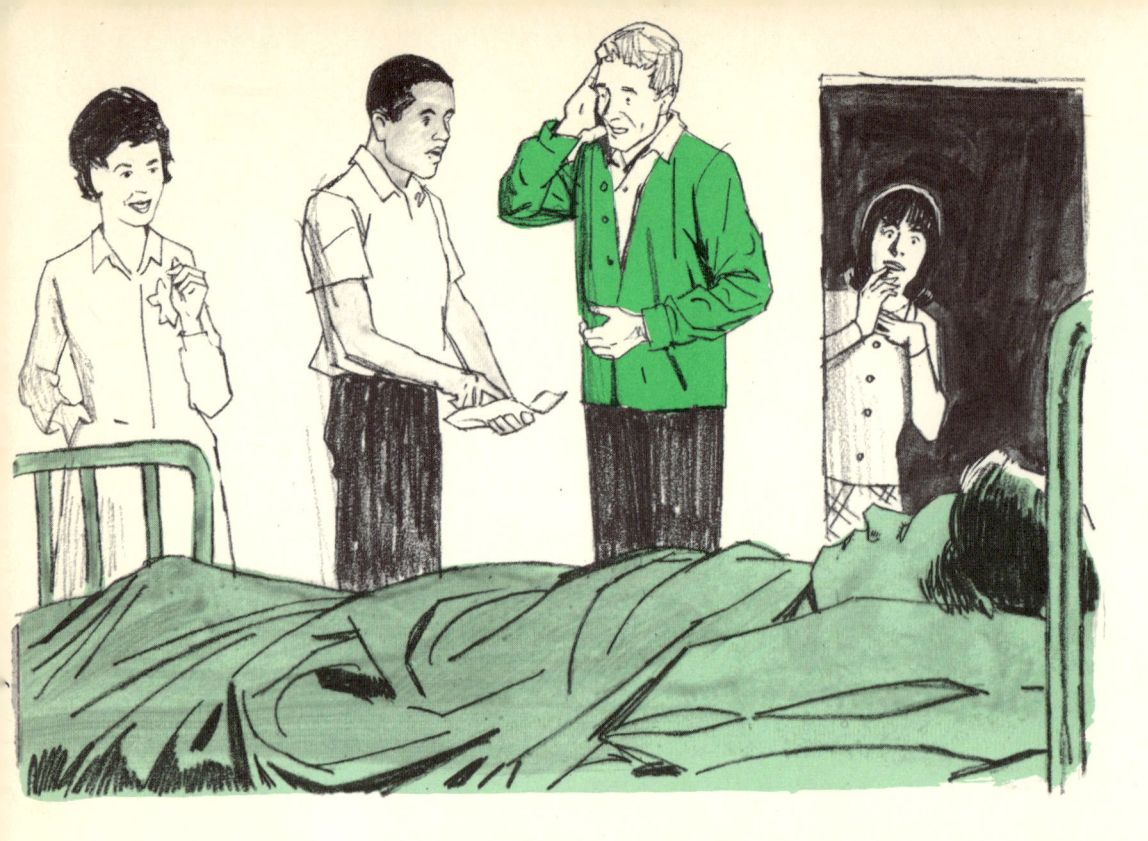

As he opened the box he said, "This is to make sure you won't spend all of your time looking at the nurses."

Mike made a move as if to raise his head.

"Now you be quiet," insisted Bumps. "Here's the set of clubs you've been waiting for. They're all yours."

"Bumps ...," Mike began.

Bumps held up his hand. "Remember, I'm your boss. I don't want you to say a word."

"Thanks, Bumps, thanks," said Mike. He shook his head slowly from side to side. He seemed unable to believe what was happening.

Mike's mother had come quietly into the room. Mike waved his hand toward the night stand by his bed.

"I think he wants me to show you something," said Mrs. Fisher. She took a piece of paper from the stand and handed it to Bumps and Chigs. It was an order blank with a note written on it.

Ace Marine Supply Company

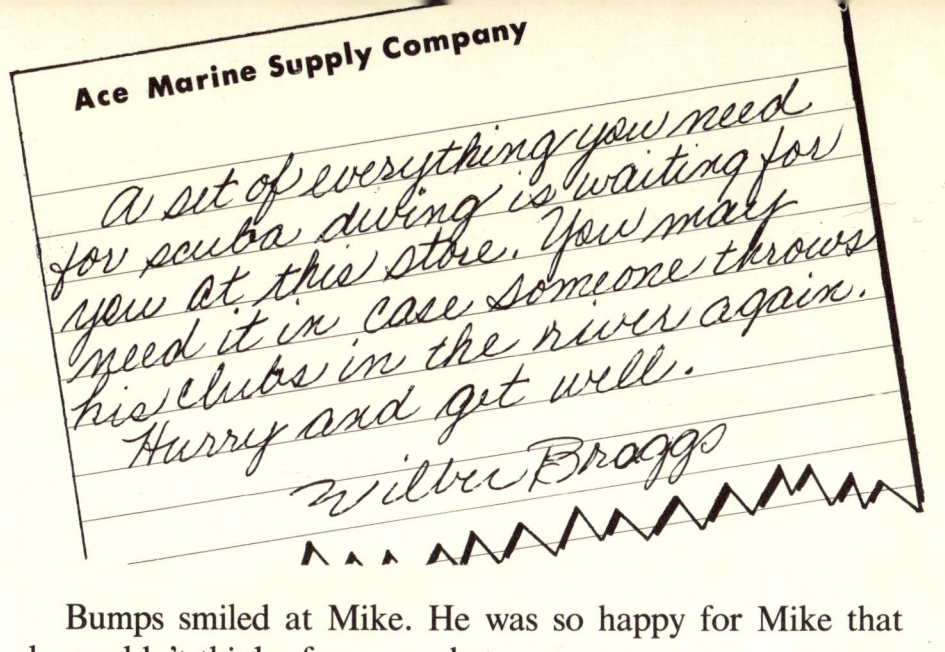

A set of everything you need for scuba diving is waiting for you at this store. You may need it in case someone throws his clubs in the river again.
Hurry and get well.
Wilbur Bragg

Bumps smiled at Mike. He was so happy for Mike that he couldn't think of any words to say.

Then Mike started to smile a big smile. "It's just like you always said, Bumps," he laughed.

"What do you mean?" he asked Mike.

"Well," Mike said, "anything that happens may be good or bad. You just have to know how to look at it."

"Time to leave," said the nurse.

Mike raised his hand in a goodnight. "Thanks again, and remember," he said, "don't take any lead nickels!"

TEN FEET TALL

Howie Brown wants terribly to be important in some sport. At Center City High School he has tried them all but is always too short. Find out how Howie finally makes it in sports and how he finds a home with Coach and Maggie Dickers.

NO TURNING BACK

Tom Hoffman, who becomes a star football player for Center City High, faces a decision at the time of the homecoming game that affects his relations with the Center City team members, the Coach, and his own family. Discover how an unexpected event solves Tom's dilemma and brings about a happy solution for all.

FAIRWAY DANGER

Mike Fisher's love of golf and skin diving leads him into mysterious and dangerous happenings at the Hickory Hills Golf Club. Read how Mike's loyal friends, Bumps Blake and Chigs Moreland, do some detective work of their own on Mike's behalf.

TIP OFF

Chigs Moreland, star basketball player for Center City High School, hopes to win a sports scholarship to State University when an accident takes him out of play. Center City needs Chigs to win the state tournament. Follow the chain of events that brings everything to a happy ending for all.

HAVILAND GRADE SCHOOL
Unified District 474
HAVILAND, KANSAS 67059